#middletonmanor

SANDRA J. PAUL

GRAVESIDE✻PRESS

CONTENTS

THE LEGEND OF MIDDLETON MANOR

The old Victorian mansion stood on top of a hill at the edge of Middleton, with only a steep walking trail that led to its impressive brass gates.

There were no concrete roads leading up to the house, not even broad sandy paths that would have once taken horse and carriage up the hill. There used to be a road long ago, but it was overgrown and could no longer be used. Only the small path gave access to the hill, surrounded by ancient trees whose roots were treacherous and thick and seemed to move as if they were alive.

Overlooking the town as though it had eyes, the

gloomy three-story building had been the inspiration to many, from photographers to sketch artists to painters to people working in the movie industry who thought this was the perfect haunted house. It had inspired many and no wonder. Middleton Manor appealed to anyone's imagination.

During the past hundred years, the mansion's walls had turned pitch black. Its windows had cracked and darkened. Its rooftop tiles were still strongly affixed but had lost their beauty. Its doors had remained shut and its gates locked. The gates' wings would not open to anyone, as if an unseen force kept them shut to the outside world. No one had succeeded in opening them, not by hand, not by machinery, not by brute force.

During the day, people walked up the path to the gates to take beautiful, yet haunting, photos. But at night, not a single soul *dared* to go up that hill. Not one. Not the toughest of tourists nor the boldest of locals. At nighttime, the mansion scared the shit out of everyone, even those who had been living in Middleton their whole lives.

During those midnight hours, the mansion lived up to its creepy reputation. Its walls would shudder, its rooftops would crackle, its shutters would bang back and forth. At night, the house lorded the town as if it was still its master.

Look at me, it seemed to scream. *Challenge me, if you*

dare. Come, take a look.

No one ever did.

But when morning returned and sunlight beamed through the clouds, things always seemed brighter. Life would pick up again as if nothing had happened, as if the windows hadn't slammed open and shut by an invisible force and the walls hadn't trembled in their foundations.

Daytime was when the tourists came in droves, either out of curiosity, or because they were eager to discover the secrets that were hidden behind the old walls. Many ghost hunters and paranormal fanatics climbed the hill, believing they would be the chosen ones who could enter the mansion after a hundred years.

Even dating back to the fifties and sixties, people stopped by the house to try to get in. Into the seventies and eighties, pictures of the house were published in various national newspapers. Books were written about it. Historians came by to explore. Building constructors brought heavy equipment that they dragged up the hill to try to get inside. No one succeeded in doing so.

The rumors about this place being haunted had first been mocked, but as decades went by, the mystery had grown and the gossip had increased, causing a frenzy amongst ghost hunters. Thanks to social media, the so-called *Legend of Middleton Manor* had taken on a life of its own.

Mostly, young people traveled to Middleton to see the building for themselves. Each and every one of them was in awe of what they saw. They took photos by the hundreds. The frenzy and hype grew.

More people came.

And more and more.

The hashtag #canyougetinsidemiddletonmanor sparked a TikTok trend that lured even more interested parties, and the local townsfolk didn't stop the rumors. In fact, they encouraged them. Tourists meant business and business was more than welcome in their town, so they—albeit reluctantly—allowed the craziness to happen so that they could rent out their houses, hotels, and B&B rooms to the visitors, who would often stay for a week to visit the beautiful area that surrounded Middleton. Although the locals weren't initially interested in profiting off the mansion, that changed when the mayor pushed a campaign about how the tourism would improve local business. And so, residents didn't stop the rumors. In fact, they started encouraging them.

In the eighties, tourist shops started popping up. First, a few small ones with some modest trinkets. Later on, many more filled their shops with mementoes and gifts like magnets, framed photos, figurines, and ornaments.

T-shirts that read *I survived Middleton Manor,* were sold by the dozen. Restaurants and ice cream parlors appeared; coffee bars thrived. Today, Middleton is a thriving town, and it's as popular as Loch Ness.

But would the people of Middleton stay happy had they known the true story behind Middleton Manor's darkness? Would they have welcomed all those who tried to enter the building, or would they have warned them to stay away?

THE MIDDLETON FAMILY

Back in 1837, when Middleton Manor was built at the request of a local wealthy man, everything seemed peachy perfect. It was created by a famous architect and the construction work took place over the course of a year. Everything went smoothly.

The man and his wife moved in shortly after and had one son. Not long after, the wife fell to her death when she tumbled down the large staircase. The wealthy man and his son stayed at the mansion, becoming self-chosen recluses, until the man hung himself, stricken by grief over the loss of his wife.

The son got married, hoping that his bride would bring new light into the manor, but darkness had already entered its walls. The house turned gloomier by the day, as if the sun could no longer find its way inside. Still, they remained.

Every night, their servants went home relieved. Every morning, they returned to discover subtle changes. The bride lost her will to live; the heir lost what remained of his smile. When the couple was asked what went on in the mansion at night, they wouldn't say.

"Just go home and leave us alone," they would say when a servant reluctantly proposed to stay with them for the night.

The couple had one son named Zachary. When he was eighteen, his mother fell down the stairs, and shortly after, his father committed suicide by hanging, unable to cope with the grief.

When he was twenty-two, Zachary married a young woman named Rachel. Deep down, Zachary didn't want to get married, but he was just as trapped as those before him, resulting in his reluctant decision to find a bride. He felt guilty when he brought Rachel back to the house, seeing the despair in her eyes the moment they walked inside, realizing that he was sentencing her to a life of sadness, fear, and darkness.

As the years went by and the nights turned darker than ever, Rachel and Zachary lived their lives without an ounce of joy and happiness to brighten their days. They let go of all the servants, not wanting them to succumb to the same despair they felt every minute of every waking hour. They decided together not to have children, mostly at Zachary's insistence that the house should perish when they did. He tried to send Rachel away, but the house wouldn't let her leave. For his entire existence, Zachary felt guilty about his wife.

Rachel and Zachary died together, but the truth surrounding their deaths has remained shrouded in secrecy ever since.

It was the town's local grocer who sounded the alarm when Zachary didn't pop in for his weekly groceries. He walked over to the local police station and asked the commissioner to check on the family.

Late that afternoon, the bodies were discovered. Zachary had hanged himself; Rachel had fallen down the stairs. It was impossible to say who died first.

That night was the first night that the house had stood empty since the day of its completion, and it was shrouded in darkness and gloom as if it mourned too. The next morning, the gates, doors, and windows of Middleton Manor were found shut, never to be opened again. Who closed the gates and why remains a mystery.

What Rachel, Zachary, and Zachary's parents didn't realize was that the house stood on top of a graveyard that had been there since the seventeen hundreds, and that the original owner had been repeatedly warned by locals not to build there.

He didn't listen.

Of course, this could also be a legend.

The police found a note near the bodies of Zachary and Rachel that read:

> *If you read this, we will be dead. Do <u>NOT</u>, under any circumstances, sell this house to anyone. Do <u>NOT</u> give it away. Do <u>NOT</u> allow anyone to enter it <u>EVER AGAIN</u>. This house is <u>DOOMED</u>. For the sake of everyone, close the house <u>FOREVER</u>.*

What happened after remains unclear to this day, but it was a fact that since the discovery of the bodies, no one managed to enter Middleton Manor again.

#CANYOUGETINSIDEMIDDLETONMANOR

"Let's do this."

Amy looked at Jack and attempted to keep back her irritation but failed to do so. Of course, her husband Jack would want to take on this challenge. She expected nothing else. He'd been obsessed with Middleton Manor ever since he came across its legend during his many research hours on haunted houses.

"Of course," she muttered beneath her breath.

Amy and Jack had heard the circulating rumors about the old Victorian mansion for years and, frankly, it scared her that her husband wanted to tackle this place next. She didn't know why, but there was something about the house and its past and present rumors that made her shiver. Pictures and stories of it sent a chill down her spine unlike anything she had ever experienced, and she hadn't even been to Middleton yet.

The whole hype hashtag thing that challenged people to go to the house and try to open the gates had to be bullshit, a setup by locals to gain visitors. Anyone should've been able to open that gate. It was stupid to believe that they were being held back by some dark entity.

Or was it?

She didn't really want to find out if there was truth behind the rumors, but she had known from the moment that Jack started mentioning the mansion on a daily basis that it would only be a matter of time before he persuaded her to make a weekend trip out of it. And she knew that she would go because she loved him too much to say no.

It was hard being married to an infamous ghost hunter and not getting involved with his passion. Jack was addicted to his profession, which was not just a job but a way of life by now. It paid the bills, and it made him happy. Over the course of the years, he'd visited several haunted locations, from castles and houses to derelict asylums and hospitals, and shared the live footage with his fans. *The Blair Witch Project* was the onset of that passion. Even though that movie was totally bogus, the idea that there were dark entities out there scaring the shit out of people never let him go, and so he started making a living from it. He started out as an amateur ghost hunter, setting up his own YouTube channel and gaining followers by entering creepy places that were talked about often. Old medieval castles, recent mansions, abandoned buildings, *The Queen*

Mary... Nothing phased him.

His followers grew by the day. He had sponsors, which resulted in plans to make his own television show, and because he was attractive as well as smart, he knew exactly how to draw the attention of a large audience. The camera loved him, and Netflix loved him too. The deal on the table was huge.

There was only one major problem: Jack didn't really believe in ghosts, entities, and dark presences. At all. He didn't start out as a believer, and his work hadn't changed that.

His original intention had been to debunk all the rumors, but he ended up shooting footage in such a way that it became suggestive, *Blair Witch Project*-style. That's what he called it, and he made fun of everyone who actually believed that there was something out there. Since he was a disbeliever, he had no issue entering places no one else dared. He had no fear, no anxiety, no stress. He didn't get the same chill that Amy did.

She was a believer.

"Amy? Did you hear me? I said: let's do this."

Without waiting for an answer from her, he took out his phone and selected the weekend when they would go visit Middleton Manor. Knowing him, by that time he would have gained enough exposure online to have millions of people follow his every move.

THE MAYOR

It was an early Saturday morning when Jack parked his dark SUV in the car lot near Middleton's church standing proudly in the shadow of the hill. The sun shone brightly, and the streets were filled with locals and paranormal tourists, as Jack called them.

What he had predicted had happened. The moment he'd announced his plans to go to Middleton Manor and try to get through its dark gates, his followers went absolutely nuts. #jackgoestomiddletonmanor became a trend and amassed a huge following as the days went by and preparations were made.

Jack had taken his cameraman, Tom, with him to livestream the event. He video-chatted several times with Middleton's mayor and had arranged it so that no one else would try to get inside during *his* weekend. In return, he promised a lot of online promotion. Netflix was on top of the event too, using Jack's visit to announce the now-signed contract deal on an upcoming series.

The only one who didn't seem so happy about it was Amy, or maybe Jack only imagined her reluctance? He couldn't tell. She usually didn't get herself involved with his work, and she most definitely did not want to enter Middleton Manor, but she had promised to be there for him despite knowing that the camera would also be focused on her while he attempted to get through the gates.

"As long as I don't have to go inside, I'm okay with anything," she had said.

Jack tried to be considerate when it came to Amy, who was a high school teacher and really didn't want to get too much exposure at all. He usually tried to keep her out of the limelight, but this was different. They had already discussed the fact that this whole Netflix thing would make her famous too, or at least to a certain extent. The producers wanted to show the human side of things, which meant that they would be filmed at home, and she would have to talk about her husband's adventures.

Jack could feel the stress radiating from his wife, but he was sure this came from the presence of the camera and followers, and not so much from the house. After all, this was just a creepy house, even when it was looming on top of the hill and unlike anything he'd ever seen before.

Even Jack, who always kept his cool, had to admit that

this place gave him the shivers. He didn't know what made this building different from the others. Maybe it was the color of the walls or the house's atypical style—even for Victorian standards—or the fact that the hill it was on was surrounded by thick, overgrown bushes and threatening trees. It was just *different*.

"I don't like it," Amy muttered as she got out of the car and stared at the dark building with something in her eyes he could only describe as fear.

A group of people had already gathered at the bottom of the hill, waiting for them. Jack wanted to ask why she would say that, but a voice behind them stopped him.

"Mr. Wilkinson."

Jack turned around and recognized the mayor, whom he had video-called with.

"Mr. Smythe, how are you?" he said, shaking the man's hand as the camera rolled.

"Good, good. You?"

"Doing fine. What a surprise to see you here. You didn't tell me you were coming."

The mayor glanced at the camera and smiled.

"Well, when you get famous guests in your town, it's important to treat them well, right? You brought your cameraman with you? I also asked one of our local celebrities to stop by."

"Local celebrity?"

"Yeah, his name is Hank White. He's a reporter. He's one of the reasons why Middleton Manor has become so famous over the last couple of years."

"I see."

Jack sighed. This wasn't the first famous location he'd visited, and he had been unpleasantly surprised like this before, but he usually made a point of telling his hosts in advance that he worked alone and couldn't afford to take anyone except his cameraman with him in order *not to spook the spooks.*

"Is it okay if Mr. White tags along?"

"Actually, if you don't mind, I really want to do this alone," Jack said. "It's my intent to open that gate and walk inside the manor with only my trusted crew member holding a camera. I hope you don't mind. It's important my followers know this isn't scripted reality *and* that you guys aren't manipulating the scene."

"Oh, but it's not his intent to go inside that house," Mr. Smythe said. "You could offer him a million bucks, and he still wouldn't do it, believe me. No, he's coming by to give you instructions before you head up the path."

"Instructions?"

"Yeah."

"About?"

"You need to know the real background story."

"Which is?"

"As you know, no one in a hundred years has managed to open that gate, but not for the reasons described online. It's important that you know more about this place and its dos and don'ts. Trust me when I say that this house is different. It comes with a manual."

"But you've never been in there yourself?"

"No, not a living soul has."

"Then how do you know?"

Mr. Smythe smiled. "Oh, I know. We all do. Mr. White more than anyone."

"Why him?"

"He's related to the family. His ancestor was the original owner's brother."

Jack smiled curtly.

"That's really interesting, Mr. Smythe, but I'm fine as it is. I don't want to be influenced by any information you give me upfront, so please thank Mr. White for his efforts. Now then, I would like to get a move on. Time is money and my followers are waiting."

The mayor looked dismayed, but Jack dismissed him and turned toward Amy.

"Let's go," he said. "Can't keep our audience waiting."

He walked toward the hill, where his followers eagerly

waited with their smartphones in hand.

MR. WHITE

AMY DIDN'T WANT TO follow her husband toward the steep path that led to the top of the hill, but she felt like she didn't have a choice in the matter. He didn't really pay attention to her now; he was already fixated on his performance. The camera followed him, his fans were actively encouraging him, people were shouting his name. He was glowing.

A media frenzy quickly unfolded. Local news cameras filmed him, and the mayor put on his happy face as he posed for them. Jack had forgotten all about her, like he usually did when he was out there doing his thing.

She didn't like these moments where he would change into a completely different person, but she knew it was part of his 'acting' (his words, not hers). She shrugged and followed him, posing as the worried but supportive wife.

He surprised her when he asked her in front of the cameras to accompany him up the hill. She didn't expect that. Usually, he didn't involve her this closely in his activities. Amy instantly felt that chill again that she had sensed earlier, and she wanted to run away, but her feet were glued to the ground, and she couldn't move.

Jack addressed the cameras.

"This is it," he spoke to his followers both physically and digitally present. "This is the moment that I go up the hill to open the gate. We'll succeed, I promise you."

"What makes you believe you can do what no one else could?" a voice called out.

Before Amy even looked, she already knew that this had to be Mr. White, the local reporter. He was in his late fifties, a gray-haired, tall, glum-looking man.

Jack turned around. "Excuse me?"

"You heard me. You don't want to do this, Jack. The house doesn't want you to. It doesn't like people like you."

"And what am I like, exactly?" Jack reacted coolly.

"A money-hungry attention seeker," White said. "The house feels that."

"A house has no feelings," Jack said, smiling.

"This one does. Trust me when I say that it won't allow you in." White's gaze shifted to Amy, and suddenly it softened. "But if you do get in somehow, which I pray to God won't happen, it'll punish you in a most cruel and destructive way. Are you willing to take that risk?"

Only Amy recognized the change in Jack's demeanor.

He was rattled but remained composed. No one else would even notice it.

"I'm going up that hill, and your ghost stories aren't going to stop me," Jack spoke calmly.

"Oh, don't worry, I won't," White said. "I'm just warning you about what will happen."

Once more, his gaze landed on Amy and there it was again: that chill. She looked away.

"Think about your wife," White spoke gently. "Go alone up that hill. Don't take her with you."

His words caught Jack's immediate attention.

"Why not?"

White didn't reply, but Amy knew that the damage was already done. Jack's curiosity had been piqued. White turned around and walked away, leaving Amy and Jack standing with the rest of the crowd.

"Well, that's that then," Jack said, grabbing Amy's hand. "You're coming with me."

The chill didn't go away this time.

THE GATES

JACK AND AMY WALKED up the steep path to the top of the hill, trailed by their cameraman, Tom, who followed right behind them. Jack casually addressed his followers, who were witnessing the live feed on his YouTube channel.

At first, it was still possible to see the people standing at the bottom of the hill while they were making their way up, but after a couple of minutes, the bushes became denser and the trees more threatening.

In front of them, the house loomed, but they couldn't see the brass gates yet as they were located on the other side of the hill. The path swerved to the right and went straight up, and that was the moment that Amy finally saw the black gates for the first time. The chill that was forever present now only intensified, and she wanted to walk slower, but Jack still held her by the hand and pulled her with him at the same pace, so she was forced to follow suit.

The house stood proudly yards behind the gates, with

shadows seemingly watching her from the inside. She flinched, which Jack didn't even seem to notice. He let go of her hand and turned toward the camera to address his audience once more with a grave voice.

"Here we are," he said. "This is it, the infamous Middleton Manor. The house that everyone has been talking about for decades. These gates have been locked for more than a hundred years. According to legend, no one has been able to open them since. Some believe that evil spirits are protecting this house. Others say that it's the oldest trick in the book: the locals somehow blocked the gates to maintain the hype that surrounds this building."

He took a deep breath to create drama and smiled bravely, flashing his perfect white teeth. Amy managed not to roll her eyes in annoyance.

"I'll show you today that either the house is cursed, or that the legend has been a setup from the start. Either way, today is the day we're going to enter the building. Should I not be able to open the gates with bare hands, I have a crew ready to go at the foot of the hill that will break through. But one way or the other, I *will* get inside this house today; that is my promise to you."

Jack smiled briefly at Amy, moved to the brass handles, pushed them downward, and pulled. Once, twice, thrice, nothing. He pushed at the gates' wings. Nothing. He pulled and shoved and used all his force until sweat beaded on his forehead.

Nothing worked, but he had obviously expected that it wouldn't be that easy.

"Amy, you hold the camera," he said. "Tom, help me out here."

The three of them switched positions. Through the camera, Amy watched Jack and Tom trying to open the gates. Again, it didn't work. Tom retook the camera, while Amy looked at the gates and the house behind it. It seemed to smile somehow in triumph. She just wanted to get the hell out of here.

"Well," Jack said, "whatever they did with these gates obviously works perfectly well. Since pushing and pulling doesn't work, I will request my crew to come up the hill with the necessary equipment to break open the gates."

"Don't bother," a familiar voice spoke.

Jack sighed audibly when Mr. White appeared in the open space. The camera fixed on him immediately. He looked from Jack to the house and then to the gate, and then finally at Amy, smiling at her with sudden sadness. She didn't understand why, but it made her want to run down the hill screaming, eager to leave this place behind forever.

"Don't you think we've tried all that?" White said softly.

"You're not the first one to attempt this, you know."

"I don't believe you did, no," Jack spoke boldly. "I believe that you've created the hype by manipulating these gates somehow. You're keeping the legend alive because it benefits your town."

White looked at him with disgust in his eyes.

"After all you've seen and read about this place, do you really believe what you're saying?"

"I don't believe that there's an evil entity residing in this house," Jack spoke boldly. "In all of my years as a paranormal hunter, I've never once seen proof of existence. You created hype that's getting this town a lot of money, but it's just that: *hype*. There's nothing to support your claims of entities or witchcraft."

"Then you're even dumber than I thought," White spat. "You're dealing with something you can't control here; don't you get that? Those few left in town with common sense have been warning others about Middleton Manor for decades. But you, with your stupid online hashtags and viral videos or whatever, are challenging the house and you've upset it. And for what? Five minutes of fame? A nice television deal? Now's your time to walk away."

Jack ignored him and walked over to Tom, telling him to stop filming. White turned to Amy and reached for her arm, forcing her to look at him.

"Don't go inside that house," he pleaded. "You *have* to listen to me. This is your last chance."

"Let go of my wife," Jack called out.

"It's okay, Jack," she said. "I'm sorry, Mr. White, I don't—"

Jack pulled Mr. White away from her. Amy stumbled backward, tripping over her own feet when White let go of her. She grabbed the bars of the gate on instinct. A loud, clear sound was heard the moment she touched the steel.

Everyone looked up.

The gates creaked and opened.

Mr. White sighed. Amy stared. Jack turned to Tom.

"Start filming again."

THE HOUSE

JACK LOOKED AT HIS wife, stunned. The gates were now fully open, allowing access to the property. For one long moment, he really believed that evil forces were somehow involved. Then he shook his head slightly. No, after all these years, he wouldn't be persuaded to suddenly believe in ghosts. That would never happen. This was all just a ruse, a setup by the townsfolk who had prepared for his arrival and the media frenzy that he would bring with him. It fit their scheme.

"Fool," Mr. White said. Jack ignored him.

"Jack," Amy whispered, "we have to leave *now*."

He looked at her.

"Are you insane? We're going in."

He reached for her hand as he had done before and was surprised at how cold it was. He leaned in, kissing her softly on the lips.

"It'll be alright, honey. There's no such thing as ghosts. You know this is all just a setup. This town needs the money, and we're just playing their game."

"But the gates opened for me. Why did they open for *me*?" she whispered shakily.

"It's what Mr. White wants you to believe. He's using a remote control or something. Don't fall for it."

"I'm not—I'm scared."

"Just like he wanted you to be. Come on. Tom, keep filming, okay? We're going inside."

Jack held onto Amy's hand as they made their way onto the property with their cameraman in tow. Mr. White didn't react.

"What's wrong?" Jack called out. "Are you scared? I thought you'd be happy."

Mr. White shook his head and remained where he was, standing safely on the other side of the gates. As Jack and Amy made their way onto the terrain, the cameraman wanted to follow suit, but before he could even walk onto the property, the steel started to crack. Both brass wings flew shut so fast they nearly crushed Tom between them.

"What the hell?" he yelled.

"Keep filming!" Jack called out. "Or better yet, give me the camera."

Tom handed him the camera. Jack turned it around and smiled at his audience.

"This is it," he said. "The moment of truth. Stay tuned."

He walked toward the steps that lead to the front door of the mansion with Amy towing behind him. When they reached the door, it flung open, almost hitting Jack and the camera.

Amy gasped.

"Remote control," Jack repeated and kept on walking, using the camera to film the inside of the house. As the two stepped through the creaking front door, a shiver ran down his spine, but he wouldn't admit to it. It was the first time he felt reluctant to walk into a building, but nothing could stop him now. This was the chance of a lifetime. Netflix would be so proud.

"We're heading inside," he said to his audience. "So far, so good."

The air felt thick and stale. It was hard to breathe. The hallway was shockingly large, with high ceilings that seemed to go on forever. The broad wooden staircase was dusty and dark. Shadows toyed with paintings and decorations. Unburnt candles were placed everywhere.

The moment they stood in the center of the hallway, the front door slammed shut.

"What the—?" Jack said.

He put the camera on the third step of the staircase, pointing it toward the door, which he tried to open. The door rattled, but it wouldn't budge. Jack dug out his phone and tried to call Tom, only to find that it was useless to even try. He checked the camera to see it was still active, which it was.

"My phone's dead."

"Mine too," Amy said. "How do we get out, Jack?"

Jack turned to his camera.

"If anyone can see this, we're trapped inside the house. We'll try to escape through a door or window."

Amy had gone silent. He knew she was upset with him for going inside the house and for paying more attention to his followers than her.

"Don't worry," he reassured her, "it'll be fine."

But he realized that for the first time, he was terrified too.

He picked up the camera. The further they ventured into the house, the darker it became. Faint sunlight filtered through the dusty windows, casting shadows across the scattered and broken furniture. The ancient wallpaper peeled off the walls in grotesque patterns that created shadows of their own. Not a single door leading out would open.

"I want to leave," Amy whispered. "Please, let's just get out of here."

"Come with me."

Jack took a brass candleholder and walked back to the

hallway, where he put down the camera again, to throw the heavy copper object against the glass door. The antique bounced against the door and fell to the ground. The glass hadn't so much as cracked.

"What the hell is this?" Jack asked.

"The devil himself," Amy whispered.

"That's bullshit, Amy," he snapped.

"Is it?" Amy moved forward and reached for the heavy object, throwing it against the glass again. Nothing. The other windows didn't crack either.

"Okay, this is weird," Jack admitted.

A frantic run through the house proved that it was the same everywhere else. They were trapped.

In a split second, as though someone had flipped a switch, all the candles inside the house ignited at once.

"Fuck," Jack whispered.

THE COLD

AMY AND JACK VENTURED deeper into the house, guided by the flickering candlelight. Jack carried the camera again, but his hands were shaking, and he had stopped talking to his audience. Amy reached for Jack's hand. His skin felt cold to the touch. Something brushed past her, but it wasn't him.

"Do you feel that?" she said.

"What?"

"The touch."

She couldn't even explain it herself. It felt like the touch of icy cold fingers brushing against her skin. Jack looked around, alarmed, as if he expected to see someone standing behind them, but they were alone.

"You're imagining things," he said.

"I'm not, and we both know it."

He didn't answer.

"We could try the windows upstairs," he suggested. "I can't imagine those pranksters tackling that area too."

"What pranksters?"

"The ones who trapped us inside the house, of course," Jack said, irritated. "I'm guessing there are cameras everywhere, watching our every move. They're probably laughing their asses off right now."

He turned the camera around.

"Are you happy now? You've got my wife scared to death. Stop this; enough is enough."

He looked up into the dark nothingness that reached far above the candlelight that illuminated the walls.

"Do you hear me? Just open the goddamn doors!"

No reply came, no change in the air, no opening of doors and windows. The silence and the touch of gentle wind on Amy's skin remained.

Jack cursed as he pulled his wife up the stairs to the second floor, where he stepped into the nearest bedroom. He stopped and, to Amy's surprise, he lowered the camera.

"There's something wrong with this room. We need to go. *Now*."

Amy pulled her hand free and took a step backward, spinning around. The door slammed shut before her eyes.

"What's happening?" She yanked at the door frantically. "I can't get it to open! Jack, help me."

He dropped the camera on the bed and tried to help

her, but the door didn't budge. The gentle touch on Amy's skin increased. The chill grew; anxiety battled its way to the surface. Fear ran down her spine, as if someone was drawing the top of a sharp blade on her skin. This was relentless, endless torment. But a thought crept into Amy's mind. She could put an end to all of this.

After all, this was all Jack's fault.

A whisper resounded in her ear, and a change in the air made her look up. Words were fed by an unseen *something* that stood next to her. She didn't even know if she could call it an entity or an atrocity, but it was there, and it would never leave her again, like an invisible devil resting on her shoulder.

He's doing this for his own gain. He set this up himself. He wants to get rid of you now for the benefit of his viewers. He's been feeding you lies. He loves his viewers more than he ever loved you.

Get rid of him before he kills you first.

Paranoia gnawed at Amy's mind. She could no longer ignore it. If she wanted to survive, she had to get rid of her husband so that she could walk out of this house. The house didn't like him. It *detested* him, but it liked her. As long as Jack was still there, the house would keep her trapped inside forever.

"Why did you want me here?" she asked coolly, balling

her hands in anger. "How could you do this? To us, to *me*, after so many warnings not to?"

He looked at her, confused.

"What the hell are you talking about?"

THE LIGHT

JACK WATCHED HIS WIFE change before his very eyes. He could see it in her demeanor, her expression, and the way she trembled, which meant that she was angry. This was no longer Amy but someone he didn't even recognize.

She was one of the calmest people he knew. She rarely got upset, almost never lost her temper, and she was always the first one to give in when they had an argument—which was a rare feat on its own, too.

But this person standing before him in the eerie bedroom was not his wife. The camera was still rolling, but for the first time, he didn't care. He cared about Amy, who was just *gone*.

His entire adult life, Jack had firmly believed there were no such things as entities, ghosts, spirits, or paranormal activity. He was dissuaded by the sheer atmosphere that lived and breathed inside this room, as if it were a person of its own. Whatever was going on was taking over his wife.

"Calm down, Amy," he said. "We have to stick together

or we're never going to get out of here."

His words seemed to anger her even more. Her eyes flashed in a darker shade, her lips trembled, her body shivered.

"Fuck you," she snapped. "Fuck you and your ridiculous ideas. This is all your fault. You're such an asshole, Jack!"

"I'm just as trapped as you are," he said softly.

"Bullshit! I *know* that you're lying to me. You've set this whole thing up. This is on you."

"What the hell are you talking about, Amy?" Jack said, starting to lose his temper too. "Calm down already."

"Or else?" she screamed. "Are you going to kill me for views and likes?"

Jack was stunned. "I—*what*?!"

"Don't even try to deny it. You want me dead, and then you'll blame it on this damned house."

"I swear I don't," he said. "You *have* to believe me. I don't understand. Whatever's going on in this place is beyond me. I'm just as lost as you are. Why would I want you dead?"

"I'm a burden to you."

"No, you're not!"

"I am," she snapped. "You've never paid attention to me; you ignored me any time I said I didn't want to come.

And you know what? I'm just as much to blame. *I've* been stupid enough to always agree with you. Well, no more."

"Amy, this is ridiculous, alright?" he said, exasperated. "Just stop this nonsense and calm the fuck down."

His words only made her snarl. She ran to the door and started banging on the wood again, so frantic and so hard that it split her skin wide open, and blood began to pour down both hands. Shocked, Jack reached for her wrists and pulled her away. She shoved him so hard that he fell backward and landed on the wooden floor. The camera hit the floor beside him. He could only imagine what his followers were saying right now.

"Please, Amy," he said, "stop it. Come back to me. It's me, *Jack*! I'm still me; you're not you right now. Look at me. It's *me*!"

Amy's eyes opened wide and feral, and she seemed to forget everything except her rage. She looked past him toward an empty spot in the room. She screamed so loud it pierced Jack's eardrums, leaving behind a ringing sound. He didn't see what she saw.

"I know," she said, ignoring him. "I know. It's him or me."

Before he could stop her, she stormed to the nightstand, picked up a candleholder and flung it at Jack's head. He barely dodged the object. He tackled Amy to the ground, holding both wrists tight until she calmed down.

"Stop it!" he yelled. "Amy, for God's sake, *it's me.*"

The door suddenly swung open again, sending a breeze into the room that chilled Jack to the bone. For a second, he thought he saw a shadowlike figure standing in the doorway, but then it was gone. The candles flickered wildly, illuminating the darkness in a way he had never seen before. He could *see* something in them, but it wasn't clear. Nothing made sense.

Amy crawled to her feet and ran into the dark hallway. A strong wind chased her, catching her hair and clothes. The candlelight seemed to follow her. Shadows appeared out of nowhere, moving past her, through her. The bedroom door creaked.

Jack grabbed the camera and threw it into the hallway, a split second before the door shut again. It landed on the edge of the stairwell, its light cutting through the dark.

It was still filming everything.

THE VOICE

Exhaustion rushed through Amy's bruised and battered form.

He's going to kill you now, the voice said. *Kill him first.*

"No," she whispered.

He's behind you. Turn around and kill him!

"No!"

"Amy, *stop,*" Jack pleaded from the bedroom.

She didn't.

She rushed to the narrow stairs and ran down the steps, going so fast her feet no longer carried her. She seemed to float, as if her body had grown wings.

Until she toppled forward.

Amy's last thought went out to her husband. At least he would be safe now.

THE STAIRS

JACK WATCHED HELPLESSLY AS Amy tore down the stairs, followed by the most horrible of snapping and thudding sounds.

The house fell into an eerie stillness.

Jack staggered to his feet, out the door, and raced down the stairs to collapse by his wife's lifeless body. Her skin was translucent; the light in her eyes was gone. Sobbing, he gathered her broken form into his arms.

Jack was broken, too. He'd lost the most important thing in his life to find a truth that wasn't even worth the battle. He gazed at the camera that balanced on the top of the staircase, facing downward, recording everything.

"It's over," he said.

A clicking sound drew his attention. The front door swung wide open, spilling sunlight into the house. Jack left Amy's body where it was. He walked brokenly to the house's front door, blinded by the sunlight. The camera still rolled, but the light flickered, as if it were about to die.

Jack turned around to see a shadow escaping Amy's lifeless body.

Stay with me. Don't leave me.

"Get out," Tom yelled.

Don't go. Please don't go.

Jack spotted a rope on the hallway floor, laying there like an invitation he couldn't resist.

A few yards ahead, the gates flew open. Tom and Mr. White stood just beyond it, gaping. They called Jack's name, waved at him. But they wouldn't move to the house. But Jack turned away, his gaze returning to the love of his life. His name was on her lips, even if he couldn't hear her speaking.

He closed the door.

COMING SOON

from Sandra J. Paul

My Truth – US, Fall 2024
Everyone is Worried — US, 2025.
The Ghost Without a Voice – UK, Summer 2025

TikTok @sandrajpaul
Instagram @authorsjpaul
Facebook @auteursandrajpaul
X @authorsjpaul

ABOUT THE AUTHOR

SANDRA J. PAUL IS a Belgian versatile author, known for her psychological thrillers and flipover novels. She has published over thirty books so far and many have been translated and are available in over ten countries. Her thriller, *Dead Girls Don't Talk*, became a Booktok hype, with rights sold worldwide to various countries. She is also a screenwriter and has sold her work to publishers worldwide.

Sandra loves anything and everything to do with the paranormal and often writes stories revolving around the subject.